My Dog Lyle

by Jennifer P. Goldfinger

Clarion Books
New York

Special thanks to Eva and Esme, my chalk-drawing artists in residence

Clarion Books
a Houghton Mifflin Company imprint
215 Park Avenue South, New York, NY 10003

The illustrations were executed in water-mixable oils,
acrylic, and other mediums.
The text was set in 18-point Matt Antique.

www.clarionbooks.com

Printed in Malaysia

Library of Congress Cataloging-in-Publication Data

Goldfinger, Jennifer P.
My dog Lyle / by Jennifer P. Goldfinger.
p. cm.
Summary: A child provides an ever-increasing list of characteristics
that make Lyle a very special dog, despite appearances.
ISBN-13: 978-0-618-63983-0
ISBN-10: 0-618-63983-7
[1. Dogs—Fiction. 2. Humorous stories.] I. Title.
PZ7.G56495My 2007
[E]—dc22
2006007146

TWP 10 9 8 7 6 5 4 3 2 1

For our dog Lyle,
who was a very good boy

My dog Lyle may look like an ordinary dog to some people. But when I was a baby, Lyle was my bed when I napped. He was warm and cozy.

My **Snuggly** dog Lyle is so clever, he knows what W-A-L-K spells.

My
snuggly,

smart

dog Lyle cries when he hears
a siren. He worries that bad
things are happening somewhere.

My
snuggly,
smart,

howling

dog Lyle wears a tutu
around his neck so he
can pretend to be a lion.
He tries to roar, but instead
out comes a *Brrrrrrp!*

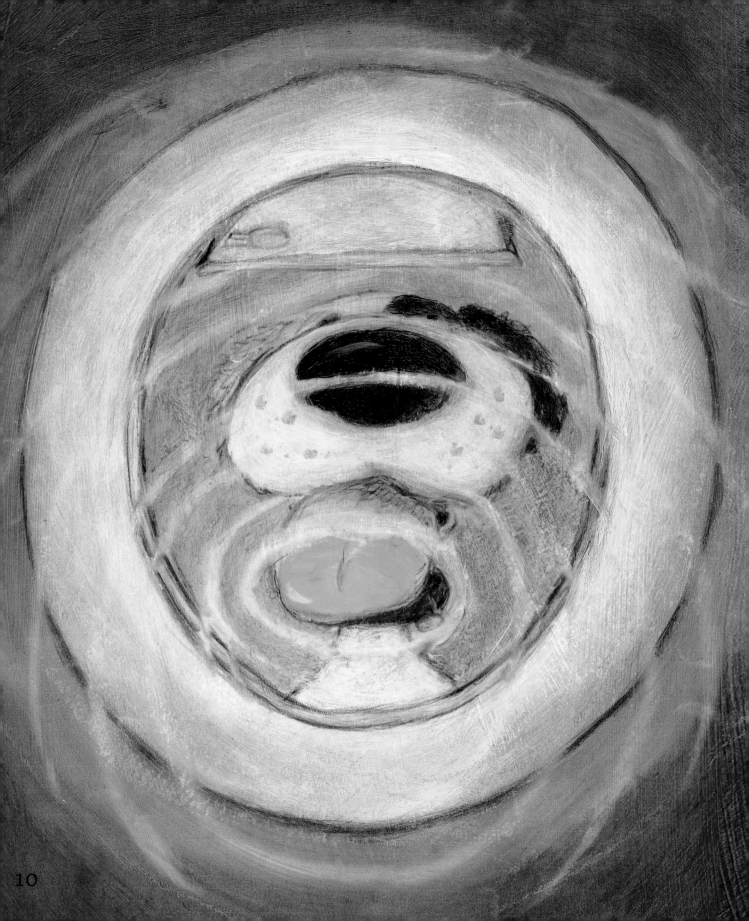

My
snuggly,
smart,
howling,

burping

dog Lyle gets so thirsty that

he drinks out of the toilet.

I try to keep the seat down.

But sometimes I forget.

My
snuggly,
smart,
howling,
burping,

Slurping

dog Lyle sometimes is

surprised by skunks.

He has to have a tomato juice

bath to get rid of the stink.

It makes him pink.

My snuggly, smart, howling, burping, slurping,

stinky-pink

dog Lyle jumps up again and again to look

over the hedge when I come home from school.

It looks as if he's on a trampoline.

BOING! BOING!

My
snuggly,
smart,
howling,
burping,
slurping,
stinky-pink,

bouncing

dog Lyle doesn't like getting his ears wet.
But when he does, he shakes his head so
hard that he sometimes topples over.

My
snuggly,
smart,
howling,
burping,
slurping,
stinky-pink,
bouncing,

Shaky

dog Lyle sometimes gets a tummy

ache and eats grass so he'll throw up.

It makes him feel better.

My
snuggly,
smart,
howling,
burping,
slurping,
stinky-pink,
bouncing,
shaky,

bellyachy

dog Lyle looks out the glass door

for squirrels that come too close.

Sometimes he forgets it's shut.

My
snuggly,
smart,
howling,
burping,
slurping,
stinky-pink,
bouncing,
shaky,
bellyachy,

Smooshed-nose

dog Lyle sits in the driver's
seat when we leave him in
the car at the grocery store.
I wonder where he would go
if he could start the car.

My
snuggly,
smart,
howling,
burping,
slurping,
stinky-pink,
bouncing,
shaky,
bellyachy,
smooshed-nose,

on-the-go

dog Lyle sneaks up to my

bed after I leave for the day.

He slips under the covers

and puts his head on my pillow.

He thinks I don't notice.

My
snuggly,
smart,
howling,
burping,
slurping,
stinky-pink,
bouncing,
shaky,
bellyachy,
smooshed-nose,
on-the-go,

Sneaky

dog Lyle is afraid of
thunder and lightning.
When there's a storm,
he hides under my bed.

27

My
snuggly,
smart,
howling,
burping,
slurping,
stinky-pink,
bouncing,
shaky,
bellyachy,
smooshed-nose,
on-the-go,
sneaky,
Scaredy
dog Lyle follows
me wherever I go.
He's my best friend.

My
snuggly,
smart,
howling,
burping,
slurping,
stinky-pink,
bouncing,
shaky,
bellyachy,
smooshed-nose,
on-the-go,
sneaky,
scaredy
buddy
Lyle may look like an

ordinary dog to some people . . .

. . . but not to me.